The Bridge Between Light and Darkness

Tanner Bergsma

Beloved Reader,

Dear readers, I urge you to wholeheartedly embrace hope. This immensely impactful book, which I sincerely hope strikes a profound chord within each and every reader, will lead you to rise above the all-encompassing anguish. Kindly take note that this book may encompass deeply emotional and devastating moments that will profoundly impact you. Prepare yourself for the intense emotional journey that awaits within these pages. May you find the resilience to navigate the profound sorrow and discover solace within the pervasive shadows that envelop this exceptional work of literature. Embrace the profound bond and realize that solitude is a foreign concept. Immersed in a sea of brilliant illumination, your heart overflows with limitless bliss as you uncover the route to true contentment in the direction your eyes behold. It is important to grasp the concept that regardless of the physical distance that separates us, my essence shall forever dwell within the innermost recesses of your heart. May you, dear reader, uncover the profound joy and radiant illumination that lies within the depths of your soul.

Sincerely,
Tanner Bergsma
Author: The Bridge Between Light and Darkness
Mental Health and Homelessness Avocate
Serving "One Voice, One Goal, One Mission"

DEDICATION

In honor of my beloved daughter, Myla, the fond hearts of Mom
and Dad shall dearly yearn for your presence.

ACKNOWLEDGMENT

I want to express my deepest gratitude to everyone who has offered their unwavering support during these difficult times. Your kindness and generosity have been beacons of light in the darkness. To those who are currently struggling, I urge you to hold onto hope, for even in the bleakest moments, there is a promise of brighter days ahead. Believe me when I say, things will get better. Together, with resilience and perseverance, we will overcome these challenges and emerge stronger than ever before.

"Follow your heart, but make your choices wisely. There will always be a bridge between light and darkness, it is up to you which path you take."

TABLE OF CONTENTS

DEDICATION   iv

ACKNOWLEDGMENT   v

CHAPTER 1   1
  Grandpas Perspective
CHAPTER 2   4
  Grandpas Perspective
CHAPTER 3   9
  Grandpas Perspective
CHAPTER 4   12
  Grandpas Perspective
CHAPTER 5   15
  Grandpas Perspective
CHAPTER 6   18

CHAPTER 7 21

CHAPTER 8 23

CHAPTER 9 25

    Alina's Perspective

CHAPTER 10 29

    Alinas Perspective

CHAPTER 11 32

    Grandpas perspective

CHAPTER 12 35

    Grandpas perspective

CHAPTER 13 38

    Mickeys perspective

CHAPTER 14 40

    Mickey's Perspective

CHAPTER 15 42

    Mickey's Perspective

CHAPTER 16 44

    Grandpa's Perspective

CHAPTER 17 47

    Alina's Perspective

CHAPTER 18 49

    Alina's Perspective

CHAPTER 19 52

    Mickey's perspective.

CHAPTER 20 55

    Mickey's perspective

CHAPTER 21 59

Alinas perspective

CHAPTER 22 60

Grandpas perspective

CHAPTER 23 62

Mickeys perspective

CHAPTER 24 65

Mickeys perspective

CHAPTER 25 67

Mickey's Perspective

CHAPTER 26 69

Mickeys perspective

CHAPTER 27 71

Mickeys perspective

CHAPTER 28 73

15 years later.....

CHAPTER 1

Grandpas Perspective

T he morning began with a reviving crispness, ushering in the first day of autumn. I found myself tucked away in the pavilion at Green Meadows Retirement Home, savoring my morning coffee as the day unfolded before me. I couldn't help but think about my grandson Mickey's upcoming visit, which is truly one of the highlights of my month. The air carried the distinct tickling sensation of fall, a feeling that danced on my nose, and as I sat there, I couldn't help but notice that the air carried the sensation. Given that I am 82 years old and that I am somewhat confined to this location, the possibility of having companionship, even for a brief period of time, was something that I eagerly anticipated. An overwhelming feeling of loneliness can be experienced, particularly during these golden years.

When we went outside, the day unfolded into a breathtaking display of beauty, with a cloudless sky adding to the already picturesque surroundings. Moments like these, with the promise of Mickey's company, added a glimmer of warmth to my otherwise predictable days at Green Meadows, despite the fact that life at Green

Meadows may be routine.

With the scent of coffee still present, I made the decision to go for a stroll, which turned out to be a straightforward pleasure that brought me a sense of peace. I was able to navigate the somewhat difficult steps with the assistance of my cane, which became a companion for me. My frail body occasionally protested by creaking and groaning. After reaching the bottom, I took a moment to pause and catch my breath. As I leaned against a nearby tree, the world seemed to completely stop moving for a brief moment. Patricia, who was the only gardener at Green Meadows, was working quickly and carefully to tend to the flowers that were lining the path. "Hello Patricia!" I yelled out, which started a brief conversation between us. Her responses were as scarce as mine, a silent understanding between two individuals who found comfort in solitude.

By way of a casual explanation for my unusual appearance so early in the morning, I mentioned, "I am aware that my grandson is going to be coming to town to visit me." Following the exchange of well-wishes, Patricia went back to her gardening, and I continued my stroll, butterflies flitting around me in a delicate dance. The path, which was adorned with daisies and pansies, led me in the direction of the sidewalk for pedestrian purposes.

After making the decision to take a detour to the left, I made myself comfortable at the base of a massive willow tree and savored the peace that surrounded me. An unexpected beauty was revealed within the confines of a nursing home by the presence of Green Meadows, which featured an abundance of flowers and towering willow trees. As I leaned against the trunk of the tree, my thoughts started to wander, and I found myself entering the realm of daydreams, which is a familiar place for me.

Not only was daydreaming more than just a passing fancy for me, but it was also a retreat into a world that I had created for myself. Some people had made a joke about the possibility that I would become disoriented in my dreams and never come back. Even though it was intended to be humorous, there was a degree of truth to it. I was able to lose track of time as I completely submerged myself in the landscapes that my mind had created.

The situation was the same today. While leaning my head against the trunk of the willow tree, I allowed my thoughts to wander, eagerly anticipating the embrace of a daydream that held the promise of discovering new stories. And this is how everything started.

CHAPTER 2
Grandpas Perspective

It is somewhat ironic that I happen to tell you about my beginning in the middle of the story, but hey, that's just how I am for you. As I began to drift off to sleep, I had visions of my wife and me when we were younger. From what I can tell, she was my heart and everything else. It was Lauren that she was. Lauren, who had the most stunning golden brass-colored hair that waved all the way down to her shoulders, was the person in question. Oh my goodness, as soon as I laid eyes on those stunning blue eyes of hers, I fell in love with them. The way it sounded made me laugh out loud. When she was out and about, she would always be seen wearing her favorite blue dress, and you would never see her wearing anything else. I never really understood why she detested everything else, but she could not stand to have anything else on her body while she was wearing it.

A miniature house with a white picket fence and white pillars that supported our house was one of the things that we had before.

We had everything, from the vintage Chevrolet Mustang to the backyard that was quite large. The fact that our children were able to grow up in this house brought them joy. Having said that, that was when they were in their younger years. After the death of my father Richard, who was involved in a truck accident a few years after my wedding, I began an unhealthy relationship with alcohol, which ultimately led to my becoming an abusive person. I regret the ways in which I responded to it because it had an effect on me. Following the consumption of all of the paychecks on alcoholic beverages, my wife relocated herself and our children to the residence of her mother. This left me to face my ugly demons on my own, with the intention of taking my own life. I really wish that I had shown a different reaction... I took some deep breaths.

Immediately after my wife left, she was involved in a car accident that took her life the following year. Both the children and I were pretty much shattered by that. On the other hand, Lauren's parents decided that they no longer wanted the children because of my intoxication and the children's defiance. In other words, the children were placed in foster care when they were seven years old. I was a drunken scumbag who was only concerned with obliterating my troubled past. I didn't care about anything else. That I never had the courage to open those unlocked closets, and they continue to be closed until the end of time. I would receive letters from the children requesting that I come and visit them, but I was unable to do so. There was a refusal to do so by Children's Services. In spite of this, the children were unaware of this. My heart broke when I saw the suffering in my children. After the age of 15, I made it a point to never see my only daughter. I was only aware of the foster home that she was placed in, it would appear. She was, in her own way, tortured, and I never became aware of the full extent of the story;

however, I lost her for good when I was 15 years old. After being overcome by darkness, she committed suicide by hanging herself in the backyard of my own home. The horror that I witnessed is something that I will never, ever forget. "Do you care about me now, dad?" was written on a note that was fastened to her noose. If I had to guess, I would have said that I had dropped the beer bottle and sat for almost four days in a row without getting up from where I was already sitting.

They left me alone after they had finished their investigation of everything that had happened. The horrifying visions that kept appearing, however, were something that I never got over. In spite of this, I refrained from touching the alcohol. My life was forever changed by the presence of her spirit. It is still fresh in my mind that I arrived home one day to find my house completely destroyed, with no apparent reason for the destruction. There was a lock on every door, and everything was shut.

Despite this, there was still a note that read, "care about me yet?" written in blood. After maintaining communication with my son Doug, I was finally able to put an end to the hauntings of Emily. One of the medications that I was instructed to take by the physician was chlorpromazine. It appeared to be of assistance in putting an end to the visions. For Emily's sake, I started looking for work, I stopped receiving disability benefits, and I assisted my son Doug in paying for his college education. Although it might not be everything, at least it can be considered something.

In the aftermath of Doug's completion of his degree, he tied the knot with Riley and moved into a red house located in the city of Stratville. Riley had aspirations of becoming a teacher, and in the end, I was the one who paid for her to complete her education degree that she had been working toward. She was doing tremendously well in her role as a teacher for students in grades 9 through 12 at the secondary school level. In addition to that, she enjoyed gardening. The white pillars of the porch would blend in with the ferns that she would hang up above the porch. She would do this by hanging ferns. When you saw it for yourself, it was incredible. I had a deep affection for both my son and my daughter-in-law. However, Doug never forgiven me for the mistakes I made when he was younger. Because he harbored resentment and bitterness toward me, I was excluded from the family relationship. Additionally, it led to him becoming an alcoholic, and he also lost his children Mickey and Alina, as well as his wife Riley. Following the removal of his children by Children's Services, Doug was in a state of despair, and he placed the blame on Riley. As a result of Doug and Riley's fatal car accident, which occurred after they had been fighting for a considerable amount of time, the children were left without a parent. When Alina's children found out about it, she did not appear to be upset in the least. Mickey was able to take it very well. At the age of sixteen, he was living on the streets and began using drugs. In the past, he has lived on the streets, and he continues to do so today.

Mickey is the member of my family that I have taken the most under my wing out of all of them. After achieving success in business, his sister Alina went on to further her education and become a successful entrepreneur. I was never quite able to comprehend the reasons behind the divergent paths that these two siblings chose to pursue, but Alina communicated with me very little during her younger years. The fact that I was completely removed from the chaos was, I suppose, of some assistance. Currently, Mickey is 19 years old, and Alina is 21 years old. My only wish is that this visit that we have today will go smoothly.

CHAPTER 3
Grandpas Perspective

I received a phone call from Mickey not too long ago, and he expressed his desire to come to me for some guidance. At this point, it was almost time for his visit, and he was uncertain about what the day had in store for him. I was climbing up the willow tree when I was involved in an unfortunate incident; I ended up throwing out my back in the process. "OUCH!" I let out an exclamation. By utilizing the tree as a support and working my way back up, I was able to successfully put my back in place, which brought about some welcome relief. The Green Meadows Retirement Home provided me with a cane, and I slowly made my way inside to the room that was designated for guests.

From the moment I stepped foot inside the establishment, I was greeted by Rose, a charming lady who extended warm greetings. She asked, "Hello, Albert, how are you doing today?" in an amused tone. In response, I offered a chuckle and said, "Visit with Mickey as usual." I took Rose up on her offer to show me the way to the guest room, and I followed her down the hallway. The hallway, which was adorned with a dazzling chandelier that was suspended from the ceiling, was constructed with cedar flooring and stretched out in an elegant manner. "Gorgeous as usual," I murmured to myself, and Rose gave me a nod of approval in response. We went into the guest room, which was only partially furnished but was essential for having private conversations.

During the time that I was expressing my gratitude to Rose for reserving a seat for me, I poured myself another cup of coffee. When I took a quick look around, I was amazed to see yet another chandelier hanging from the ceiling. The quartz in the chandelier caught the sunlight and completely transformed the space. My attention was drawn back to the sound of footsteps coming from behind me as I was lost in admiration. "Hi Grandpa, how are you?" The arrival of Mickey, my grandson, was seen. "Hi Mickey, how are you?" I extended a greeting to him. During our conversation, I noticed that he had a medium build, was wearing corduroy jeans that were torn, and was wearing a black muscle shirt that was covered in tattoos. I couldn't help but compliment him because his appearance conveyed a great deal of information.

I inquired about the reason for his visit because I was intrigued by the topic. A deep sigh came out of Mickey's mouth as he opened up about the difficulties he has been experiencing ever since his sister Alina moved to Chicago, leaving him feeling abandoned and disoriented. He was experiencing a great deal of pain, and it was reflected in his eyes. "I am so sorry," I said in a sincere manner. His continued disclosure of his struggles with self-harm and depression caused my heart to ache for him when he continued.

The words that Mickey's father had spoken earlier prompted

him to seek the guidance of someone who had traveled a path that was comparable to his own. After acknowledging that we had experienced the same thing, I found that I was having a difficult time coming to terms with the fact that our histories are repetitive. "It is true, yes," I admitted, inviting him to share his burdens with me. The story he told about living on the streets, surviving, being depressed, and being confused struck a chord with him, and he pleaded with someone to comprehend and assist him.

His distress moved me to reassure him that he was not the only one going through this. I knelt down next to him and urged him to look into my eyes, despite the fact that our experiences were vastly different and the years that had passed. "It will be okay," I assured him. My heartstrings were pulled by his vulnerability, and it brought to mind the significance of maintaining connections with others.

As I stood up, I proposed that we indulge in some food before delving into the past. I was surprised to find that I did not have an appetite for the macaroni and cheese that Mickey was eagerly digging into. At this point, it was time to face the specters that remained from the past.

Chapter 4

Grandpas Perspective

W hen everything that happened took place, I was just a young age. A tranquil and peaceful place where life was good could be found in the small town of Stratville, which had a population of only about 15,000 people all together. I was placed in a foster family, which was a quiet yet hardworking family, after being adopted. In spite of the fact that she had a wonderful passion for food, my mother was frequently short-tempered and impatient. She worked as a waitress. Due to the fact that she was a manipulative and dishonest person, there was never any trust between us. When he was not working as a general laborer in a steel factory, my father enjoyed being in the presence of blueprints and, in his spare time, he was frequently seen riding motorcycles. My parents, on the other hand, frequently butted heads when it came to the subject of child rearing. Throughout the day, they would argue and bicker with one another, which would eventually escalate into yelling matches that were extremely detrimental to the dynamic of the family.

A good school, an elementary school where there was a lot of drama, was where I received my education. Yet, just like in every other school, the teachers made an effort to instill a positive morale in each and every student by encouraging them to "be the best you can be." During my younger years, I was unable to accomplish this goal. I remember being a child who was relatively reserved and cautious when I was in the second grade. Jacob, my brother, on the other hand, was a delightfully outgoing individual who took great pleasure in making other people laugh. After participating in a talent show for students in grade 2, he even attained the distinction of being named the year's best "kid comedian." Everyone had a good time. Because he was the more outgoing of the two of us when we were younger, he developed into a more daring and adventurous child.

But when I turned eight years old, things started to go from bad to worse. Both a stoner and an alcoholic, my father was a stoner. On a daily basis, he would return home from the bars, smelling terrible, and his breath would smell like rubber tires due to the fact that he would smoke hash and weed. When I made a mistake, he took the strap and repeatedly beat me with it. He did this throughout the entire process. When I was a child, I experienced feelings of both fear and hurt. In her spare time, my mother would use heroin, and she was perpetually in need of financial assistance. In order to make up for it, I would frequently discover that the house was always occupied by a man whom I would never know. It wasn't until much later that I discovered that she was selling herself for money.

There was a worsening of my father's alcohol problems when he was ten years old. Due to the fact that he spent his entire paycheck on alcoholic beverages, we were never able to afford food or rent for the house. In addition to being starving and never being fed, my family was evicted when I was 12 years old, and my parents divorced. My mother's health deteriorated over time, and she ultimately passed away from an overdose. As a result, I was left with no other option but to reside with my abusive and alcoholic father. When I was 14 years old, I weighed only 70 pounds per year. During my time at school, I was called a variety of names, including "skinny meat sack," amongst many others. I eventually went to the house of my neighbor in order to get some food, and when she ran out of money due to an addiction problem, I decided to search through the garbage cans in order to find some food.

I was taken away and placed in a shelter that is known as The Roof and Protector, or T.R.A.P. for short. This happened after a concerned local citizen called Children's Services and requested that they take me away. The T.R.A.P. was present to safeguard children who had been removed from the care of Children's Services. In spite of this, I never felt secure there. In a period of time that was less than six months, I was subjected to physical assault, robbery, and became addicted to jib. After escaping from the shelter when I was 16 years old, I made my way out into the streets to start a new life. I was heading in the direction of destruction without even being aware of it because I was a teenager who was impulsive and never gave things a second thought. That being said, despite everything, I was still determined to live.

CHAPTER 5

Grandpas Perspective

T hen why did my great-grandparents behave in such a cruel manner?" While Mickey was sipping his tea, he remarked, "They appeared to me to be so innocent and kind." The sauce had even splattered across his chin by the time he finished his final bite of his meal. Despite the fact that I did not have complete certainty regarding this question, I did know one thing.

"They had their own problems, and their parents never treated them in the best of ways," I explained further.

"I never got to know my parents a lot, as I was always wrapped up in my own problems."

"You know... I was never able to comprehend this insane family." Mickey let out a sigh and said, "With the exception of my sister, we were never especially good at getting life." It was never something I wanted for myself, my family, or anyone else. "Why is it that your Great-Grandpa and Grandma are experiencing the same issues that you and I are? It's almost as if a curse is following our family around."

For a long time, I pondered this. When I was younger, I, too, did not comprehend the situation. However, there is a phenomenon in life that is referred to as "repeating history." Mick appeared to be perplexed. In a state of bewilderment, he inquired, "What do you mean by repeating our history?"

"When I say that we all learn from what we are taught by the parents around us, which is what I mean when I say that we repeat history. Rather than learning from what other people say, we typically learn from what other people do and the circumstances that surround it. What we go through and how we are treated both contribute to our learning. Believe me. Due to the fact that this is how I was taught, I ended up becoming addicted to both gambling and alcohol. Your father gained knowledge not from what I said but rather from what I did. However, he continued to love you."

Like air in a balloon, Mickey tightened his muscles. As I watched him struggle to hold back his tears, I could see that he was becoming increasingly angry. He yelled out, "I'm not talking about this part!" His only concern was for himself, and that was the only thing that mattered to him.

When I heard the pain in his voice and saw the trembling in his chin, I felt compassion for him. "Please accept my apologies, Mickey. I do understand. Your father was completely oblivious to the issue. I failed to be the kind of father I ought to have been to him, and there was a lack of attention that I paid to him. Yes, he did have options available to him. It is my gift to you. However, he did not learn from what I said but rather from the experiences that he had. This is how he learned to cope with the pain he was experiencing. I took it out on him, and he took it out on you because of it. It wasn't until much later in life that he realized this for himself. Your parents' passing does not mean that he did not love you, even though they are no longer alive. He felt a deep affection for both you and your sister. It is not in his best interest for you to feel sorry for him or to model your behavior after his. Both he and I want you to deviate from the traditional pattern. I explained that this is our highest hope."

"I am on my way out. Now is not the time for me to deal with this," Mickey got to his feet, thanked the nurse, and then departed. The reason that Mickey reacted in such a manner is not entirely clear to me; however, when I was a kid, I used to behave in the same manner. It is not an easy topic to discuss, I am aware of that. However, I am aware that he will be required to carry out the task in order to achieve happiness and, for his own sake, to save his life.

CHAPTER 6

I t is beyond my comprehension why my grandfather is speaking in such a manner. It's utter nonsense, as if he is insane for claiming that my father still loved me. I feel sick to my stomach just thinking about him saying that his father cared. The fact that I was alive or dead was of no concern to either of my parents. I was physically beaten with a strap almost every day when I was five years old. In addition, they constantly yelled at me, called me names, and brought me down to the point where I attempted to kill myself by using my father's antidepressant medication. Nevertheless, it was unsuccessful. For what reason could my parents ever love me? Things have a very different feel to them now that they have passed away. There is a sense of calmness about it.

Alina, my sister, was always making fun of me for being stupid, and when I was in elementary school, she spread rumors about me that were completely false. That was another use for the strap that my parents had. My grandpa has the audacity to tell me that my parents loved me, and the level of anger and hatred that I have toward them is absolutely astounding. What an absolute load of nonsense that is! He has never, ever put himself in my position! What was he doing to look out for me? It is almost as if my entire family is not on speaking terms with me at the moment, and I suppose he was the only one I spoke to, but he does not appear to care about the situation. Exactly like my own father. It seems that my father had a nice example to look up to. I gave a sigh of relief. I suppose that the fact that he is no longer alive is supposed to make things better in some way.

After leaving the nursing home, I made my way down the winding path that was curved. I stomped on the ground as I walked away. That was a pleasant sensation. To a certain extent. My suffering seemed to go unnoticed by those around me. I am by myself alone. I am entirely alone. There is no one. My point is that nobody cares!!!! A level of anger that was so intense that it made me want to punch a tree. Yes, I did. Although it was painful, it was somewhat satisfying. I continued to punch and punch until there was a significant dent in the tree, and my hands were covered in blood and raw. It was both stinging and very good. I felt exactly the same way about myself as I did about the pain. It was able to dull the pain somewhat. It gave me a sense of satisfaction in a way. I understood the level of hatred that they had for me, and I felt it for myself as well. I couldn't contain my emotions for much longer. All I wanted to do was scream. It is to yell at another person. All that was present, however, was nature and nothing else. I saw a squirrel who was not too far away from me. While I was on the ground, I picked up a stone and hurled it with all of my strength. It landed on the ground a few yards away after striking the squirrel in the chest and knocking it to the ground. I made my way to it, placed it in my bag, and then turned around and headed in the direction of the northeast, toward the forest that I considered to be my home.

CHAPTER 7

Being homeless is a life experience that can completely deplete you of all your resources. It is as if you are beneath the lowest of animals, even beneath pigs, and everyone else is above you. Pigs are still treated with a certain degree of respect, despite the fact that they have a reputation for being filthy. Pigs are provided with food and warmth, and when it comes to their ultimate fate, at least it is handled in a humane manner. When compared to this, the reality for those of us who live on the street is very different. Instead of being treated with respect, we are spit upon and called insulting names such as "faggot" and "loser." Both of these terms are frequently used. It is clear that we are not being treated on an equal footing, and this inequality is palpable. When I talk about pigs, I can't help but bring up the insulting term that we use to refer to law enforcement officers. Simply by being present in a store, they appear to have a tendency to look down on people who live on the street, as if we are engaging in some sort of inappropriate behavior. On the other hand, the police do not question a businessperson who is well-dressed when they enter the building. We are the only ones who are treated in this manner; why is that the case? If we are considered to be the lowlifes that we are, is that a fair assessment? Considering that we are also human beings! It is disheartening that other people are unable to comprehend the challenges that I have faced. Even though Grandpa believes he comprehends, I have my doubts that he actually does.

Since the tender age of five, I have been subjected to abuse at the hands of my alcoholic father. When I returned home each day, I discovered him in a drunken stupor, and he had neglected to provide me with food or care because he was so drunk. I had to try to feed myself when I was only five years old, and every time I did so, he would lash out with his strap, yelling and hitting me in a manner that was reminiscent of the Roman habena that was used on Jesus. As I approached the eighth grade, my weight had dropped to a mere 70 pounds, and the scars that were caused by the strap were visible on my back. There were no friends in my life, and I felt like I was trapped inside my own house. I was isolated. In the end, Child and Family Services (CAS) entered the picture, but the situation continued to deteriorate after their intervention. My residence was taken away from me, and I was transferred to the Herringdale Nursing Home. After being subjected to malnutrition and abuse for a period of six years, I made the decision to flee, which ultimately led to my current circumstances.

I retrieved a squirrel from my bag, which was mangled as a result of an earlier encounter with a rock but was still fit for consumer consumption. While I was setting up my tent in the woods, I made the decision to start a fire. Following the preparation of the squirrel and its consumption, I made an effort to fall asleep by basking in the soothing warmth of the flames. The weight of my experiences feels like it is too much for me to bear, and I wonder how much more of this there is that I can take.

CHAPTER 8

I n spite of my best efforts to fall asleep, I kept having flashbacks while I was lying down. The unexpected text message that I received during one of my school days simply stated, "You need to call home." You see, I was surprised to receive it. It is only the act of dialing the phone and making the call that I can recall. I came to realize that it was the worst day of my entire life.

Mikael, I am at a loss for words to convey this information to you," they said. To which I replied, "Just say it." "I am unable to," they finally said. My voice became more trembling as I urged, "Just say it." Your mother and father have just passed away as a result of a truck accident, Mikael. Accidental death occurred on the highway as a result of a collision with a tanker. When I think back on it, all I can remember doing is turning that desk over, escaping the classroom, and punching and pushing anyone who was in my way. Due to the excruciating pain and agony, I felt the urge to rip my heart out of my chest.

I awoke because I was unable to remain still and sleep. My mind was racing. Why did God choose for this to take place in my life? By that point, I had lost all sense of emotion. I had been mistreated by them throughout my entire life; therefore, why should I care? It took me a good two hours of running before I realized that I had arrived in a different city. It was my desire to torment these cities and make them experience the same anguish that I did. There is a knife in my heart every time I take another step, and I hope that one day, people won't turn their backs on me or ignore me. There was a flood of tears in my eyes, and I was at a loss for what to do. I dashed across the bridge and peered over the edge of the structure.

Immediately, without any hesitation, I dove headfirst into the darkness.

As soon as I opened my eyes in the medical facility, the flash-backs went back to me. As I lay in bed, I pondered the following questions: why am I still alive? Why am I not dead? The agony is beyond what can be tolerated. I hear a nurse entering the room. She said, "You're going to be okay," as she placed something freezing on my knees and head before leaving. "I won't worry about you." Due to the fact that the lights were out, I was unable to see what she was doing. I was awake for what seemed like an interminable amount of time. However, I believe that life is simply more enjoyable when it is completely dark. I am currently in an icy and dark place, and it is likely that I will remain there for the rest of my life.

CHAPTER 9

Alina's Perspective

When I open my eyes, the time is nine o'clock in the morning. Particularly for this time of day, the sunlight that is coming in through the window appears to be exceptionally bright. Despite the fact that I am aware that today is going to be a momentous occasion, I get out of bed and proceed with my usual morning routine. I have a very important business meeting scheduled with the board of directors of Sophinka, which is a company that I co-founded and oversee with my friend Belinka. The meeting is scheduled to take place at twelve o'clock in the afternoon. By virtue of my position as president, it is my responsibility to ensure that the various functions of the company are carried out in a seamless manner. Although my job entails a lot of different aspects, the primary focus of today is to make a convincing argument as to why a company with a market capitalization of 5.5 billion dollars ought to invest in our clothing line.

Sophinka is a fashion retailer that caters to a wide range of fashion requirements, providing a wide range of products, including models, high-end suits for a variety of occasions, elegant dresses and attire for both men and women. My mind is free to wander into the realm of daydreams as I begin my day with a cup of coffee. The anticipation for today's presentation is truly exhilarating, and I am looking forward to it with great excitement.

When I think about the "what-ifs" of life, I often find myself wondering how different things might have been if my parents were still alive or if my brother had chosen a more prudent path, avoiding the influence of our grandfather, who is a loser. In the early morning hours, the city of Chicago, where I currently reside, appears to be especially captivating. Despite the fact that I have to leave as soon as possible, I take the time to relax on my balcony and take in the peaceful atmosphere.

As I finished my coffee, I was confronted with the harsh reality that I was running behind schedule. After hurriedly going through my apartment, I dash out to my car and make a beeline for the meeting that is about to take place. I am hoping that the members of the board are not also delayed, and my thoughts are racing through my head. After a brisk ten minutes, I finally made it to my office, which is located in the center of downtown Chicago. As soon as I walked into my workspace, I sat down in my chair and opened the emails for the day. Among the regular requests for additional invoices and reminders to make payments that Hydrotex sends, there is one message in particular that catches my attention. It is a note from Sherry, who was previously married to my brother.

Dear Sister,

In the saddest time of my life, I am about to reveal something to you, and normally I should be happy. But since your brother, Michael, left, I have not been the same. I am going to say this. I have had a headache and was really nauseous this morning, to the point where I was throwing up. I have meant to tell you this for a long time, but with Michael leaving, it has been hard on me. I am getting nervous as I write this, but oh well, here goes nothing. I am 3 months pregnant with your niece, a beautiful girl to whom I have decided to name Myla. I tried to find your brother, but I couldn't. Please tell him to come home to his family. He has a baby girl on the way, I need him home.

I apologize for writing to you in your work email, but I had to as I could not find your phone number. I look forward to hearing from you soon.

Sincerely,

Sherry

Because I was experiencing a peculiar combination of happiness and shock, I found that I was at a loss for words. Another piece of information that came to my attention was the fact that my brother had completely abandoned this girl. Taking into consideration that he was my brother, this revelation was perhaps not entirely unexpected. At the same time that I was closing down my email tab, I joined Sophinka, who was wearing one of our luxurious dresses. It was a silky black velvet gown with a frilly hem that exuded sophistication.

I complimented her by saying, "You look absolutely stunning today," and she responded with a straightforward "Thank you." As someone who is reserved and reserved by nature, Sophinka really shone when it came to coming up with new ideas for fashion concepts. Together, we went into the room where the board was meeting, and we took our seats at the head of the long table. However, by the time thirty minutes had passed, there was still no one else present. It was at this point that I felt the beginnings of frustration, which compelled me to go to my office and check my email.

An email that I had hoped to avoid discovering was discovered by me, much to my dismay. It was Dr. Scott, the head investor, who delivered the news in a manner that was terse and straightforward. I am sorry to inform you that after careful consideration, we have come to the conclusion that we are not interested in investing in your company at this time. Thank you for your understanding. Our best wishes are extended to your company for success in all of its future endeavors.

Unable to find the words to express my frustration, I slammed the door on my computer and left my office. The burden of dissatisfaction continued to weigh on me, and I was aware that I could not go through another day like this.

Chapter 10
Alinas Perspective

When I woke up the following morning, I was experiencing a notable lack of health. A surge of anger erupted within me as I merely considered the possibility of losing the investment deal, particularly in the absence of an understanding of the factors that led to its failure. Taking into consideration the extensive amount of effort that I had put into our company; from designing to making connections, all the way to meticulously preparing the presentation, this unexpected rejection felt especially impolite to me. I sought solace in my bed, drowning in the melancholy tunes of Adele, whose heartbreaking songs seemed to amplify my distress. I was frustrated by my apparent inability to comprehend the complexities of these situations, and I sought solace in my bed.

While I was lying on my bed for what seemed like an eternity, the constant ringing of my phone broke the solemn atmosphere that I had created. My decision to not respond was based on my lack of interest and disconnection. During that particular instant, I was experiencing a strong desire to put some distance between myself and everyone and everything. This feeling prompted me to contemplate withdrawing into a state of isolated despair. When compared to confronting the harsh realities of my professional setbacks, the allure of oblivion appeared to be more appealing. After the melancholy soundtrack of Adele's ballads started to get on my nerves, I threw my phone against the wall in an attempt to get rid of the frustration I was feeling. The force of the impact shattered its delicate facade, but my indifference toward the material damage was a reflection of my indifference toward the world.

I was overcome with a pervasive sense of depression as a result of the fact that I felt abandoned by my family, who appeared to be emotionally distant. I longed for nothing more than the comfort of my family, but the emotional toll that I had been forced to bear over the course of my life felt intolerable. Although I was unaware of it at the time, the decision to transform this hopelessness into productivity turned out to be a pivotal moment. I decided to ditch my pessimistic demeanor and put on a bright red jumpsuit before going for a jog through the well-known paths of Lincoln Park.

Running turned out to be a therapeutic escape for me, a way to alleviate stress and confront the inner turmoil that I was experiencing. My reflections were set against a serene background that was created by the winding pathways that were decorated with the vibrant colors of autumn leaves. As a means of bringing some lightheartedness into my otherwise gloomy disposition, I decided to make my jog into a game I could play. My objective was to make my run an oddly satisfying pursuit by attempting to synchronize my footsteps with the falling leaves. Because of the transformation of the leaves into a breathtaking tapestry of red, gold, and brown, my surroundings provided a momentary reprieve from the struggles that I was experiencing on the inside.

During the course of my run, however, I came to an unsettling realization about two hours into the run. It seemed as though an old Volkswagen was following me, which was a disturbing presence that contributed to the development of a sense of paranoia within me. Despite the fact that I changed my route, the silver Volkswagen from 1979 continued to be there, with tinted windows that concealed the identity of the person who was driving it. The feeling of unease became more intense, which prompted me to make a hasty trek back to the security of my apartment.

After arriving at my front door, the circumstances took a turn that I had not anticipated. I was surprised to find that my apartment had a surprise waiting for me when I opened and closed the door behind me. As I was walking to the restroom, I stood in front of the mirror and absentmindedly brushed my hair from side to side. In the midst of this precarious situation, an unexpected event took place: a man in his mid-30s appeared before them, brandishing a baseball bat. Before I had a chance to comprehend the threat that was developing, he struck me, which caused me to fall into darkness.

Chapter 11

Grandpas perspective

I discovered that I was profoundly concerned about Mikey and that I was heartbroken. I was left bewildered by his unexpected departure from the meal, and I was unable to comprehend what could possibly be going through his mind at that moment. At the same time that I acknowledged that he had every reason to be angry with me, the suddenness with which he left raised some concerns that I was concerned about. What happened to him? My thoughts immediately went back to the unforgettable recollections of what had occurred to Doug, my son. I may have let him down, but I was resolute in my commitment to not let my grandchildren down, either. Suddenly, I was filled with the determination to fight for them.

As I pushed away the remnants of my meal, I picked myself up from my seat with a renewed sense of determination. The tenacity that was still burning within me as an old fogey was something that I marveled at. I knew that I had to fight for my grandchildren until the very end, despite the fact that my body was showing signs of wear and tear. Even though I knew the journey would be difficult, I decided to take on the challenge.

I was able to make my way back to my room by using the walls as a support while I navigated the corridors. There, I adorned myself in the business suit that belonged to my late father, which brought back memories of a time when I was wielding a different kind of sword. I made my way to the safe after gathering my sunglasses and, yes, my gun among my belongings. I was drawn to my stunning golden cane as it caught my attention with its glint in the sunlight. Many people were unaware that it was not only a cane but also a sword at the same time. A secret that I had effectively concealed. I was a member of the Queen's guards in Britain when I was younger. I was skilled in sword fighting and other forms of martial arts. I learned jousting, a skill that I detested, and I honed my shooting abilities at gun ranges during those days. I also learned how to shoot effectively.

As I stepped outside, I discarded the regular cane and grabbed hold of my golden cane instead. An old Volkswagen from 1979, which I affectionately referred to as my "Volksy," served as a symbol of my heart and pride. As a result of a momentary lapse in memory, I was unable to locate my car keys; however, I was able to quickly rectify the situation by discovering that they were hanging from my security chain.

My mind was flooded with memories of World War II as I inserted the keys into the ignition of one of the vehicles. Before I became a member of the royal guard, I was a veteran who fought alongside Freddie, who is a close friend of mine. My friend and I flew together during the Battle of Britain, and we were affectionately referred to as "Lil Skipper." My thoughts continued to dwell on the unfortunate passing of Lil Skipper, the sight of my classic Hurricane fighter plane, and the camaraderie that I had experienced. I was holding tightly to the old locket that he had given to me as a gift; it was a treasured memento from a treasured friend.

After waking up from my daydream, I concentrated on the here and now. I was determined to locate my grandchildren and make sure that they were safe, so I sped off as soon as the engine started roaring to life. Even though the path that lay ahead was not entirely clear, the determination to safeguard them was stronger than it had ever been.

CHAPTER 12

Grandpas perspective

I drove my old Volkswagen at a high rate of speed down the highway, leaving the marshy areas behind and entering the plains of Michigan from the west. As the hours passed, I pondered the possible locations of my defiant teenage self and the possible places she might be. In the event that I was attempting to avoid being discovered, where would I go? My mind was flooded with memories of camping trips that I had taken with Doug, and I recalled the locations that we used to go all the time. We would either go fishing by the shore of Lake Michigan, where we would cast lines and catch fish, or we would go fishing near the grounds of Toronto, where the CN Tower would tower over us. I was so preoccupied with my thoughts that I drove until the arthritis in my feet started to hurt. When I was almost ready to pull over, I had a sudden realization: my granddaughter had mentioned something about a clothing line in Chicago, more specifically, a place called Ikram. That is the possible location of her! However, before I could proceed, I had to find my grandson. That is, if I could only locate him.

While I was thinking about it, memories of a campground called Riverside Park came to mind. Doug and I had been there quite a few times, but the question that remained was whether or not Doug had ever brought Mickey there. Because it was only twenty minutes away, it was a distance that he could easily travel to get there. I sped up on the Fisher Fairway, and after going by the Woodmere Cemetery, I arrived at Riverside Park in less than twenty minutes. I stepped out of my car and started walking, thinking about the various locations within this vast park where I might be able to find Mickey.

In addition to marshes and shrubs, Ponderosa Pines were also present in the grassy landscape. As I turned my head to the right, I noticed that the Spokane River was crossed by a massive suspension bridge. My eyes caught sight of him as I stood in the middle of the bridge.

When I saw Mickey standing there, a figure in the distance, I felt a wave of relief wash over me instantly. As I moved forward, my pace quickened, and with each step, I got closer to my grandson. As I got closer, a flood of memories came racing through my head; they were memories of Doug and me exploring this very park.

By the time I reached the bridge, the feeling of melancholy was overpowering.

"Mickey!" The sound of my voice reverberated throughout the vast area as I yelled out. When he turned around, our eyes met, and his gaze conveyed a sense of simultaneous surprise and recognition. We stood there, suspended in a moment of reunion, feeling as though the past and the present were being brought together.

As Mickey approached me, I noticed that he was resembling his father, Doug, and I was able to confirm this observation as he got

closer. Doug possessed the same spirit of adventure that had char-
acterized his youth, as well as the same twinkle in his eye. During
our embrace, a mutual understanding was passed between us in si-
lence. The burden of worry was lifted, and it was replaced by the joy
of discovering a piece of family in a location that was completely
unexpected.

We sat on that bridge for a considerable amount of time, rem-
iniscing about the years that had passed since we had last seen each
other. While Mickey was telling stories about his life in Chicago,
where he was pursuing his passion for fashion, I was telling stories
about Doug and the adventures that we had encountered in Riverside Park. The bridge evolved into a metaphorical connection between different generations, serving as a demonstration of the un-
breakable bonds that remained between us despite the passage of
time.

During the time that the sun was setting below the horizon,
casting a warm glow over the park, I came to the realization that this
unplanned journey had not only brought me to my grandson, but
it had also brought me to a location that was replete with memories
and the echoes of a history that we both shared. Riverside Park, with
its Ponderosa Pines and expansive landscapes, served as a backdrop
for the reunion of people from the past and the present, which
served as a demonstration of the tenacity of personal relationships
within families. We were able to remain connected to one another
through the bonds of love and the unwavering spirit of family as we
stood on that bridge beneath the waning light of the sun.

CHAPTER 13
Mickeys perspective

I decided to take a walk down to the park. Dad always used to take me down here when I was younger. It was a beautiful day with an ocean-blue sky and fluffy white clouds. Fields of dandelions line the grass, but somehow, even with all the beautiful nature it still made me really depressed. I am not sure why. I just can not stand being on the streets anymore. I am so tired of it. I walked further up the path and onto the center of a long suspension bridge that towers over some sort of lake. I have no idea, but my mother would have known. She used to take gardening pretty seriously, I remember her coming up to me once and asking me to put a hydrangea bush in the front garden... and oh boy, did I ever make a stink about it. I hated getting my hands dirty, as I like to consider myself "pristinely gorgeous" as being part of the LGBTQ community. I loved just sitting on the chair and watching my mom garden. My sister loved teasing me about how I act too much like a girl. Well, I mean in my defense, I wore skirts and dresses sometimes... But who cares? I mean... I used to like it... then. Part of me still wants to, but the streets are a whole different ball game. As I stood on the bridge, something loud, like a banging noise went past me. (Must have been a truck on the nearby highway or something.) But my PTSD kicked again, and I found myself flashing back in the dimensions of time.

CHAPTER 14
Mickey's Perspective

Taking a stroll down to the park was the plan that I made. When I was younger, my father would frequently take me to this location. The sky was a crystal clear ocean blue, and the clouds were fluffy and white. It was a beautiful day. The grass was covered in fields of dandelions, but despite the fact that it was surrounded by such stunning natural scenery, I found myself feeling extremely depressed. It is not clear to me why. It is simply intolerable for me to continue to be out on the streets. It is taking its toll on me. Continuing my ascent along the path, I eventually arrived at the middle of a lengthy suspension bridge that was suspended over a lake of some kind. What I don't know is that my mother would have been aware of it. When she was younger, she used to take gardening very seriously; I remember her approaching me at one point and asking me to plant a hydrangea bush in the front garden... and boy, did I ever make a fuss about it when I heard about it.

Despite the fact that I am a member of the LGBTQ community, I do not like getting my hands dirty because I like to think of myself as "pristinely gorgeous." It was so relaxing to just sit on the chair and watch my mother tend to the garden. Whenever I acted too much like a girl, my sister would make fun of me and make fun of me. In defense of myself, I should mention that I occasionally wore dresses and skirts... What does it matter? That is to say... In the past, I used to enjoy it... The streets are a completely different ball game, but there is still a part of me that wants to do it. I was standing on the bridge when I heard a loud noise that sounded like a banging sound from behind me. There must have been a truck on the highway in the vicinity or something like that.) Nevertheless, my posttraumatic stress disorder (PTSD) manifested itself once more, and I discovered that I was experiencing a flashback in the dimensions of time.

Chapter 15
Mickey's Perspective

In the streets, I became a member of a gang that was known as Rebels on Wheels. In the beginning, everything was going swimmingly! For a brief period of time, I was under the impression that I was Mr. Kingshit, complete with all of the gold necklaces, attractive women who would do anything to have me, and a life that was perfect. The kind of person who dealt out the jib and the shrooms and made thousands of dollars was me. When I was younger, I would go to the bars every night in order to get inexpensive drinks and to meet the prostitutes. Everything was fine at first, but that changed when a member of the human resources department betrayed me. It would appear that within this group, whatever you produced was shared. The problem, however, was that I did not keep my stash after I had made it. During the time that I was standing in the bar drinking, I had already consumed seven shots from my bottle of whiskey when this individual, who we referred to as Big Chuck, sat behind me. He had a long beard that must have weighed 300 pounds of pure muscle. He had a powerful beard. He placed an order for his own bottle of whiskey, took a few sips, and then turned his attention to me. He says, "You know, we true members of ROW do not support people who are snakes, rats, or lying ballers."

He is referring to the participants in the ROW. I was sitting there when he stood up, took another long swig of his whiskey, and then smashed the bottle against my head. I fell apart completely. Attempting to get back up while dazed, I felt hot pokers go inside my back, and I screamed in pain as they went through my anatomy. I attempted to stand up despite the excruciating pain I was experiencing when another blow struck my back, causing sharp pains to travel through my spine. I was helpless to move after hearing a crack in the ground. People were shouting, "Amor y Respeto! ROW," and I heard them. It meant "love" and "respect" in his native Spanish. An assurance of commitment to ROW. After that, a series of blows struck my sides, and when I lay dormant, I was struck again. I was abandoned, helpless, and in a great deal of pain. During the time that I was crying, I allowed the darkness to gradually consume my body.

CHAPTER 16

Grandpa's Perspective

M ickey was yelling and crying uncontrollably when I approached him. I went up to him. But I went up to him and attempted to give him a hug, even though I had no idea why he was acting in this manner. Like a wild boar, he continued to flail his arms in a wildly erratic manner. His PTSD episodes are the only times he reacts in this manner. My curiosity is piqued as to what the cause of this is. In order to comfort him, I simply hold him and give him a gentle hug. After some time, he loses his composure and comes to his senses. His sobbing, on the other hand, does not cease. Grandpa, he mutters to himself. I suppose that I will never grow out of my role as a parent. As I looked at Mickey and gently wiped his tears away from his face, I said, "It's okay, Mickey." then I looked at him. "I am also aware of the location of your sister." He is no longer crying. Do you agree? Indeed, he inquires. "Yes, I am able to. If you are interested in going on a short road trip, then we should go together. Our arms were linked as we made our way down the stairs together as if we were two ducks that were hanging from the ceiling.

Eventually, we are able to get into the car, and we make the decision to go to the one location in Chicago where I knew she was.

The two of us, Mickey and I, are relatively quiet as we drive. After much deliberation, I made the decision to listen to Linkin Park, which is Mickey's favorite band. We are traveling down the fairway in an old Volkswagen while Chester Bennington is singing his headbanger song "numb." Mickey begins to sing "I feel so numb..." and before I know it, we are both singing "I feel so numb..." and the rest of the song. I started to sing along with Mickey. Mickey turns off our speakers at the very end of the show. One of the things that he says is, "It's funny how we are saying that we are feeling so numb, yet you are driving, and I am on my phone." We both laugh at the same time. By the time night falls, we have arrived in Chicago. As we are both thirsty and hungry, we make our way to a Mickey D's and pull up to the drive-through window. Nevertheless, I overhear Mickey saying something as we are placing our orders. Look at me, Grandpa. In the direction that Mickey was pointing, I turned my head and looked over. There was a young lady traversing the path. This silver Volkswagen, which was almost identical to mine, was parked behind her.

Mickey received the food that I had gotten for us. As I was taking out my binoculars, I thought to myself, isn't it true that every grandpa has one? A closer look was taken by me. Waving long hair, hold on... The closer I look, the more. She wears a locket on her wrist. What appeared to be... Could it be that? Indeed, it was! Hello, my granddaughter! "It's Alina," I introduced her. "How are you able to tell?" Mickey inquired with a curious tone. In response, I say, "That amulet belongs to her mother." "What the hell are you talking about? I don't see a locket anywhere in sight. Also, why in the hell do you have binoculars in your possession? Mr. Mickey says.

"Because these are of military grade, I am able to spot a mouse from a distance of 150 yards... and in addition to that, I proceed; this is how I am able to see her amulet. Don't let go, Mickey; things are going to pick up speed very quickly. I accelerated the car and drove in her direction. She entered her apartment, but it appeared that someone was already inside, and the situation was suspicious. She went inside her apartment. When I say, "Let's go up and look," I ask. Mickey warns his grandfather not to stay in this area because there is a possibility of danger. "Why am I unable to..." My pause "Excuse me!" Mickey said as he hurriedly exited the vehicle in order to visit his sister. Due to the fact that I am in a precarious situation, I made the decision to make myself comfortable and get ready for what seemed to be the longest days of my life.

CHAPTER 17

Alina's Perspective

As I open my eyes, I am greeted by a strange pounding sound between my legs. I let out a scream as the pain is excruciating. There was an occurrence. I had no ability to stand or see. While the man is lying there, he is thrashing his pelvic region into mine, and I can hear him moaning. My attempts to stand up were unsuccessful because he had me bound, gagged, and blindfolded. I was unable to let out a scream. Suddenly, I find myself crying uncontrollably. Subsequently, I experience a sensation similar to fluid flowing into me; the man exited the vehicle content and only briefly glanced in my direction. "At this point, you will be carrying my child, and if it turns out to be a girl, I will treat her in the same manner that I treated you," she said. He stated this as he stood up. I screamed for assistance as he attempted to untangle me. I am utterly disgusted by you. While crying, I let out a yell. It is a laugh. "Yes, I really do wonder what caused the failure of your business deal...the reason why your brother is sick, the reason why your family is lost, and the fact that your family is so messed up in general..." He comes to a halt and dashes towards the exit. This, however, is too late.

47

In the moment that he opens the door, there is a man who I could never have imagined standing there. My brother was standing right here, and I have no idea how he came across me. Not only did he look better than ever before, but why did he have so many tattoos? Just as I was about to say something, my brother interrupted me and interrupted me. "So you've made the decision to attempt to rape my sister?" He yelled. "The guy just stands there, not even caring about my brother and giving the impression that he is afraid of him."According to what he yells, "Go down to hell, you bloody scoundrel!" The sight of my brother pulling out his knife fills me with dread as I sit there. It is my intention to cut off your twig in order to ensure that you never rape another girl again, especially not my sister or my niece!!! While he was pinning the guy to the wall, he yelled at him. I am filled with dread as I watch him brandish a gun, shoot the individual in the twig three times, and then cause the individual to fall to the ground. I failed to look for the subsequent section. The only thing I can see is that the screaming from this guy is still going on when I reveal it five minutes later. When I open my eyes slightly, I am immediately overcome with fear. Oh my god, what is that all about? Here lies the man, who is obviously dead and covered in blood all over his body. I did not even bother to look at his fork. Oh my god, my brother was serious about this. After sensing the presence of my brother next to me, I jumped and began to cry. "Be quiet. During the process of unbinding me, my brother whispered, "It's okay." As soon as he did, I immediately collapsed into his arms and proceeded to cry my heart out. Though I was relieved to see him, I couldn't help but feel horrified and traumatized at the same time. It is as if he is picking me up and carrying me out of the scene. All of a sudden, I find myself in a state of complete darkness, and I have no idea what took place.

CHAPTER 18

Alina's Perspective

A month has passed, and it appears that I am making some progress toward recovery. I was residing in the apartment that my grandfather had discovered via some means. To a greater extent, my brother and I appear to have reconnected over the course of the past month. Despite the fact that he occasionally steals my dresses, I continue to make fun of him for wearing dresses, which appears to no longer bother him. In spite of the fact that I never understood why he would act in such a manner, I no longer cared about it. Nevertheless, there was something that continued to weigh on me. My business partner became the sole owner of our fashion design company after I had been absent from the company for a month. She terminated my employment without providing any prior notice, with the assistance of her directors, of course. However, I was too preoccupied with being happy for my brother for that to have any significance. I demonstrated the email that Sherry had sent to my brother. The news appeared to blow his mind, and he shed tears. I have no idea what caused this child to cry up so much.

Is it possible that he experiences an estrogen imbalance? I am completely clueless.

He had a habit of crying over the most insignificant of things. Nevertheless, since that time, he has been handling the news more effectively, and he has even managed to keep in touch with her through various social media platforms. Initially, I was thrilled for him, but now my excitement has increased even further. Not only is it my birthday today, but I couldn't be happier about it. I danced into the bathroom to style my hair after I had finished adorning my rainbow dress, which was the one that my brother had persuaded me to purchase. Following my exit, I made my way down the stairs. My brother and my grandfather had already taken their seats, and breakfast had been laid out on the table for them to enjoy. In the course of my exploration of the feast, I discovered quiche, sausages wrapped in bacon, orange juice, and fruit salad. What a delight! Once I had finished hugging both my grandfather and my brother, I went ahead and took a seat. Just as I was beginning to take pleasure in my quiche, my brother became distracted by a phone call and exited the room. "Who could it possibly be?" I pondered. After fifteen minutes had passed since his return, Mickey followed him into the room, his expression changing to one of shock. After making the announcement, he hurriedly went outside, and I followed behind him. "My daughter was born, and she is sick," he disclosed.

While I was standing in the doorway, I was able to observe Mickey's face, which was displaying a range of emotions, including joy, concern, and an underlying shock. Despite the fact that his daughter was a new life entering the world, she was accompanied by the burden of illness. Every one of us was affected in a unique way by the news that lingered in the air. The room was filled with a variety of feelings, including celebration for my birthday, concern for

Mickey's daughter, and a silent acknowledgment of the unpredictability of life. I was able to sense all of these emotion combinations.

My brother came back to the table in an effort to maintain a lighthearted atmosphere, which he did in an effort to strike a balance between the contrasting events. After that, we continued eating our breakfast, the flavors mingling with the emotional undercurrent that was present. Mickey received some words of comfort from Grandpa, who, in his usual stoic manner, acknowledged the bittersweetness of the situation and offered some words of condolence. We came to terms with the gravity of the situation, which resulted in a change in the celebration that we were having that day.

It was a stark reminder that life does not always go according to our plans or expectations and that the contrast between happiness and sadness was so palpable. A birthday that was marked by an unexpected twist weaving a complex tapestry of emotions that went beyond the ordinary, was the birthday that was celebrated. During the course of the day, I couldn't help but think about the intricate dance that is life, where happiness and sadness frequently waltz hand in hand, leaving an indelible mark on our hearts.

CHAPTER 19

Mickey's perspective.

I was shocked. My daughter was just born, but she is sick. I was outside on the bench in the park alongside a river. I was staring into space, not knowing much what to say. I had a newly born daughter. I am a father now. But not to a healthy girl. She was sick. I felt so helpless. I didn't know what to say or to expect. But I knew that life was going to get better. I had some faith that she was going to be better. I stared at the cygnets following their mother. The mother swan swam with her head and body gliding gracefully through the currents. It made me think about how much of a family I always wanted. Even though my family may be broken up, and I hardly ever speak to them, perhaps with my daughter, I could set a better example. The swans disappeared around a bush. Then I felt my phone go off. I wonder who this may be. Unknown caller. "Hello," I answered. Out of all the people, it was not what I expected. "Hello, this is Dr. Shadow from McMaw hospital. I have bad news.

Your daughter is getting really sick." I was completely shocked.

"Is she okay?" I ask. "I'm afraid not. She has really high acidity in her blood, and we are completing blood transfusions as we speak." Dr Shadow stated. "I will be there as soon as I can," I said and hung up the phone. I called my ex-wife. "Sherry, head up to the hospital now! Our daughter is sick! I yelled and hung up the phone." I slammed my phone down, yelled to grandpa and my sister that we needed to go, and ran to the tree, karate-chopped the stupid piece of wood down. I then ran to the car door and slammed it shut as my grandpa and sister rushed in. "What's the issue?" Grandpa yelled in frustration. "Don't slam my car door!" He said. I got snappy. "MY DAUGHTER IS FUCKING DYING, I DON'T GIVE TWO SHITS ABOUT YOUR STUPID CAR DOOR!" I slammed the car in reverse so fast that I made the luggage from the back hit the front seat. "Why the hell are you going at such speeds!" My Grandpa yelled. "HOLD ON!" I yelled. I shifted gears into drive and drove so fast I could not even see out my window. I continued for 30 minutes, until I heard sirens behind me. I cursed. Last thing I need. I pulled the car over, ran out the door, and slammed it.

"MY DAUGHTER IS DYING, YOU PIG! I DON'T CARE WHAT SPEED I AM GOING, YOU CAN GIVE ME THE TICKET AFTER!" I ran back to the car, started up, and just as I was about to pull over, I saw the police car go in front of me. He was trying to clear the highway for me and started speeding down that highway, which seemed faster than Michael Schumacher, a world-winning race car driver. My Grandpa was petrified, but I didn't care. I pulled off the shoulder of the road and sped the car at full speed, surpassing 200 kilometers an hour. I didn't care. With my grandpa screaming, which hurt my ears, I raced my way to McMaw Hospital, located in the center of Toronto, Ontario. Sherry and her family were there before me. They left two hours before I did. I guess I was too busy punching trees and dealing with my pathetic grandpa.

CHAPTER 20

Mickey's perspective

I slowly walk into the NICU. Even though they told me my daughter was sick, I had this unforgettable doubt that she was going to pass. I didn't know though for sure, but my anxiety and emotions were through the roof. I walked into the NICU slowly. There were many babies all over the place, some with their parents doting on them. Before I get to my daughter however, Dr. Shadow pulls me and Sherry into a room. "Thank you for coming," she says. I get this sinking feeling. "What's going on with our daughter, I say." The doctor's smile went grim. "I have bad news...." she stopped. She looked at both of us before continuing on. "I am here to tell you that with your daughter's condition, she is not going to survive." That's when I jumped up and snapped. "What the fuck is going on! I yell. What has gotten her to this state? WHAT DID WE MISS?!" Sherry starts crying. "Unfortunately, your daughter has a hole in her intestines, and is causing high levels of acid in her blood." Dr Shadow continues.

"We did multiple blood transfusions and have seen no signs of improvement, only worsening, which is extremely abnormal. This shows us that essentially her whole gut has died." Now I lost my shit. "Are you seriously telling me that you have done everything? What about the brain scans you promised from her having an IVH? What have you guys done about the hole in her heart? NOW THIS!" I screamed at her. It made Sherry cry even more. "Leave us fucking alone," I told the doctor. Sherry's mother tried to go near me, and I pushed her away. I wanted to be alone right now. I couldn't handle this. I walked into the NICU and passed a few babies until my jaw dropped. The fucking nurses had the nerve to be sitting around my daughter just laughing like nothing's going on! The nerve! I found a nearby trolley with medical supplies and picked it up, sending it flying tight across the nurses' station. All the nurses and Dr. Shadow just stopped laughing. At least now I got their fucking attention. "Now you fucking listen," I yelled. "HOW DARE YOU SIT THERE AND LAUGH WHILE MY BABY DAUGHTER IS DY-ING! WHAT'S WRONG WITH YOUR MORALS AND VAL-UES?" "Get out," Dr. Shadow said in a cold sneering tone. "Over my dead body will you ever," I said more aggressively this time. "You cold, callous rats can go eat donkey ass," I said. I walked up to my daughter. The nurses just walked back. There she was. As fragile and weak as anything. I ordered the nurses to remove the bassinet lid. I was trying to fight down tears in my eyes. I put on my sunglasses as to not let those stupid rats see my pain. Sherry and her parents walked in. "What happened here?"

Sherry's mom asked, looking at all the damage that the trolley caused. "Well, your stupid son-in-law just threw a trolley at us," Dr. Shadow sneered. "What a father figure," the doctor said. "What are you doing here?" I heard a middle-aged Pakistani woman in her 40s walk in. Great, another doctor. "I told you to get out of here, you were fired," this Pakistani woman continued. She looked at us. "My name is Dr. Qureshi, I will be your doctor." Dr. Qureshi looked at the reports and flipped at Dr. Shadow. "Get the hell out of here, Dr. Shadow," she said coldly. "Otherwise, I'll have you up for infanticide charges." Dr. Shadow's face went into outrage. "You wouldn't dare!" she growled. "Get out....NOW!" Dr. Qureshi snapped. How satisfying it was when Dr. Shadow and her team finally exited the room, like puppies with their tails between their legs. Nice. Dr. Qureshi looked at my daughter. "Oh dear. I hate to say it but Dr. Shadow has done too much to this poor gaffer. She won't even make it another 10 minutes.... in order to make her pain much less, we should take her off life support." The doctor's words hit me hard, but I knew deep down that she was right. One look at Sherry and she nodded her head. Her eyes were beat red from all the crying. "Ok then," Dr. Qureshi said.

She picked our daughter up and put her in my arms. Me and Sherry instinctively just interlocked our arms and held her together. About 10 minutes passed with us both saying our goodbyes. Sherry could not hang onto her anymore; she was an emotional mess. So she handed Myla off to me. I held onto her. She was squirming, but I tried cradling her back and forth. "Are you ready?" asked Dr. Qureshi. I nodded. I watched her as she took the breathing tube out of Myla. Myla was squirming and then lay still. I held her little hand, telling her how much daddy and mommy loved her. One second...two seconds...three seconds...time slowed down. Just as time did, her little heartbeat did too. Four...five...six seconds.... I counted for almost a minute until her heartbeat just stopped. I knew she had done it. No time to cry I thought, don't cry... don't cry... I fought those tears so hard. Why did something like this have to hurt?

About two minutes passed, and the doctor walked back into the room. She took out her stethoscope and listened to Myla's heart. "She has passed," she said. Sherry just left the room crying hysterically with her mom and her family chasing after her. I stayed back. I gave Myla to the doctor and slowly walked out of the room. She was gone, and so was part of me.

Top of Form

CHAPTER 21

Alinas perspective

A fter the death of my niece, I couldn't understand it. Why did she have to die? I just held Sherry as she ran out of the hospital. My grandpa was busy talking with Dr. Sherry's mother. I decided to talk with Sherry. I didn't understand any of this; not a single bit. I walked out of the NICU and down the steps to the back parking lot. It was relatively quiet down there until all of a sudden, I heard a fire alarm. I didn't understand what was going on. First it was Myla, and now apparently a fire? I grabbed Sherry's hand, and we ran past cars and outside. We made it to the parking lot safely. I looked around. I couldn't see grandpa or Mickey. "Grandpa? Grandpa!" I yelled. After about 5 minutes of shouting, I felt a hand on my shoulder. I jumped and shrieked. I turned around, and there was my grandpa and my brother. I was happy. At least they made it out alive. But all of a sudden, my brother ran off towards the burning hospital. "Mickey! ..... MICKEY!!!" I yelled in between sobs. Now I was going to lose my brother. I couldn't take it. I collapsed, and my world went black.

CHAPTER 22

Grandpas perspective

My grandson ran into the burning building to save people. I couldn't understand why he would do that. My granddaughter fainted, and there I was trying to perform CPR. I called for medics. Luckily, there were plenty of them at the hospital. Just as I managed to get her heart going, the doctor came along and did some examinations. "She is due," he said. "Your granddaughter is pregnant and is about to give birth." I didn't understand. My Alina did get raped... Oh crap, that's why. No time to think. I left Mickey to fight the flames, and together with my granddaughter and a team of doctors, we rushed into an ambulance to the hospital.

Midway into it, though, the ambulance ran over something, making the wheel flat. Here comes grandpa again. I rushed out of the back of the ambulance and up to the driver's side. "Get out of the driver's side," I said. As he did, I hopped out of the ambulance and found 15 packs of gum in my pocket. Oh boy, I am getting old. I gave gum to all the doctors and ordered them to chew. They all looked at me funny and did. Once done, I asked them to spit it out and give it to me. I had to eventually yank one out of a nurse's mouth. Then, I gummed up the hole in the flat tire. "That's not going to do crap!" said one doctor. I just looked at him and laughed. "You will see," I said to him. I got into the driver's side of the ambulance and ordered everyone, and I got us to the hospital after speeding on the main drag and doing at least 10 minutes doing a wheelie with the ambulance. Once we got there, everything went as planned. Alina gave birth to her daughter Crystal. As we stayed in the hospital, Alina was asking about Mickey, where he was, but because she hit her head on the parking lot, she lost some memory. "I worry for him, but I know that he is doing a good thing."

CHAPTER 23

Mickeys perspective

After the death of my daughter, I walked slowly to the parking lot, in shock and despair. Suddenly, I saw a bright light and the whole right wing burst into flames. Without hesitation, I ran into the burning building. People were fleeing and screaming, nurses were busy trying to get people out. I pushed my way through the burning building and busted the door down with one kick. "Fuck this fire," I thought. My daughter may have died, but I am not afraid anymore. I got nothing else to lose. I ran to the staircase and saw a mother crying with her baby. "Hang in there," I said. I took hold of her arm around my neck. "What are you doing?" asked the woman. "Just hold tight," I replied. I lifted her up with her baby and ran down the stairs. A burning timber fell in front of me. I had no choice and without hesitation, I jumped over it. All I felt was my eyes and lungs burning, but the pain felt oddly satisfying.

I landed with both feet on the bottom stair, and I bolted right for the door. I ran out into the parking lot where it was safe. I didn't even hesitate. I ran past the door straight towards the parking lot. I put the woman and her baby gently on the ground. I ran back. "Where are you going?" the woman asked. I didn't respond. I just ran back inside. As I ran past, I noticed a Dr. Shadow on the top floor of the NICU with a dozen babies. She was terrified. "Help! Help!" she yelled. I thought about how to get up to her. There was a nearby building, the CN Tower. I guess I didn't have much choice.

The firefighters were trying to fight the fire on the west wing as it spread throughout the entire hospital. I ran to the CN Tower, got into the elevator, and as no one was looking, used ammonium and gas to cut right through the top of the elevator. I climbed up onto the top. I cut some cables, and voila, that bastard lifted so fast in the air it almost sent me flying down the shaft. I rose to the top in under 5 seconds. I jumped out into the air, and landed on the floor, cutting some cables as I did, making the elevator fall but enabling me to get about 15 feet of the cables. With these cables and a few steel hooks I happened to have in my pocket, I made a makeshift grappling hook. Nothing fancy, but it works. I tied one end of the grappling hook to one of the cables in the elevator shaft.

I then ran and with one punch, I broke the window of the CN Tower. I then jumped and in midair threw the hook. It luckily attached itself to the NICU's balcony railing. I then fell so fast it made me almost want to throw up. But as I did, the cable I was hanging onto caught my fall. Then when everything seemed fine, all I felt was a give from the other end of the cable, and I fell. Luckily the hook braced the fall, but I was sent falling at speeds I'm sure were well over 90 km an hour. I went into the wall of the burning hospital headfirst. I felt sharp pains on my nose. I must have broken it. At this point, I noticed a helicopter from above. It was the news. Oh boy. Now I have the news on me. Damn. I looked down and about

100 people, 50 police cars, ambulances, and firefighters were strewn all across the parking lot and on scene. A scream got me off guard. Just as I turned my head back, fire burst above the ceiling just behind the NICU. I ran out of time. I grabbed that cable and climbed myself as fast as I could to the top of the balcony. I barely made it on time when I realized a baby was still in the NICU. I ran inside the NICU and grabbed the baby. Screaming and crying she was, as I ran out of the NICU, and just as I did, a helicopter from a nearby hospital came to help. It lowered its basket, and just as it did I had two babies, twins, in my arms. I looked down at them. "One day, you will grow up and be good fathers, and be anything unlike me." I handed them to the paramedic in the basket. In about 2 minutes I had all the babies and the nurse inside the basket safely.

"Go," I said. I knew I ran out of time. The nurse looked back, expecting me to get in. "You won't have room, JUST GO," I yelled. The paramedic looked terrified, gave the motions to the pilot, and I watched the basket go off into safety. I turned around. Now it's my time. I just watched the flames get closer and closer, until suddenly I let the balcony give way underneath me from extreme heat, and all of a sudden here again I was falling. Falling at lightning speed, with my last vision of fire and falling pieces of brick and concrete. Then light went into darkness.

CHAPTER 24

Mickeys perspective

I wake up, but not in the same way. Here I am, I guess in spirit form. I walk past the medics and stare at my dead body. Well, I am as good as dead now. My face was half burnt. I walk slowly and look around. Medics yelling orders, sirens blazing, people on death's door. When a person died, I see their spiritual light go to the clouds, away from earth. I see another person, but this time trying to steal a purse from a woman. In attempting to do so, he clenches his chest and falls to the ground. His light comes out of his body, and something much different happens this time. He is consumed by the dark void and disappears. I wonder what is up. I continue to walk, but as I do, visions change around me. I am now in nothing but light and empty space. I am standing, but frozen. Then I see something. "Daddy." Daddy. I look around. There, standing about a foot away from me, is a girl, no more than 19 years of age. Black hair, sparkling blue eyes, and dressed in a white dress. Who is she? "Daddy, I am here," she says. ".....Who a..are... you?" I stammer. I am frozen and petrified of where I am. She comes closer and puts my hand in hers.

"I am Myla, your daughter....this was the future me," she says. "I don't understand... I say...where am I? What's going on?!" I panic. She holds my hand firmly. "Look dad, you may not know me well, but listen to me. You will have a choice to make. I love you, just be careful. There is a bridge..." She stammers off. The scene shifts, and I fall into the darkness.

CHAPTER 25
Mickey's Perspective

I landed in some strange place. I regain my surroundings. I am in this strange place.... I am on a bridge. I am standing on this bridge, with solid light on one side and solid darkness on the other. This bridge is gray, made from what seems like gray ash. I now see an angel in the light, with an extending hand. But I turn my head the other way. I am now faced with another hand coming out of the dark void. This void is dark, and this hand is nothing like I saw in the movies. It is as hellish as hellish gets. It is not even made of real matter but made from the darkness of evilness. Human blood and sin form the hand, nothing more.

"Come with me to where you will be safe," I turn. The angel is speaking to me. I guess somehow I can hear her speak. "Come with me to where you will find happiness and beware of the other hand. You have a choice to make. The other hand is made not of human flesh but of pure evil and wickedness. It's your choice to make, eternal life or eternal torture and hell." I now understand. So I guess this is what life is. The other hand stretches out even longer. "Come with me," the voice says. "That disgusting voice of light is nothing but lies....you can have everything you want with me." The angel moves closer, and its light brighter, the hand of evil moves its darkness closer. Just as I am going to make a choice, the bridge collapses. And then I see light.

CHAPTER 26

Mickeys perspective

I woke up not knowing what happened. Light was all around me. I didn't know what happened. I woke up to people. Where was I? I regained consciousness. Standing over me was my sister Alina. "What happened to you? You almost died," she says and starts crying. I took her hand. Look. We all have decisions. I made mine for a reason. There is something... I faltered off. I decided to keep silent about my visions about Myla and the bridge. I now understood. "How long was I out for?" I ask her. She looks down. About 4 years, she says. Grandpa ....passed, and I now have my daughter Crystal," she continues on. "I miss him. What if I could have saved you? You could have seen him..." Alina starts crying.

"Look sis,... I say...we all have decisions. We can either choose the light or darkness. Or we can never make a decision and never move forward in life. Life is a lot like a bridge.

How we choose to cross it on the other hand, well, that's only for each person to make." She looked surprised, then made her usual sassy comment. "Well, at least you chose not to die, and since when did you become smarter?" she says. I chuckled back. "Not since when I got smarter, or since when you became more receptive to my lecturing ass" I say jokingly. We both laugh until her phone starts ringing. "Hello," she says. The grin just wipes away from her face. My what? MY WHAT?! CRYSTAL IS IN THE HOSPITAL? IS SHE OKAY?! After a couple of minutes, tears roll down her face, she throws her phone and collapses crying. I need to make it to the hospital. She whimpers. "Let me drive you," I say. "Are you bloody ridiculous?" She asks between sobs. How can you help me? You're injured. "Look at me," I say. I get this weird feeling to peel back all the bandages and I do so and stand up. I get up with ease. "Well," I say, "the angels have their ways." Alina just looks up at me in shock. "What the...." She loses her voice and her jaw drops. "HOW?!" She asks. "You were all bloody 15 minutes ago and dead! HOW THE..." she falters off. I just say to her, I guess I made the right choices. I say. "We don't have time to waste." I take her arm over my shoulder, and run to the car. I ignore the yelling nurses and doctors. I run and spot a convertible. Perfect. I run on, put her inside, jump on the other side, hotwire the car, and as soon as I know it, we are speeding off toward the hospital.

CHAPTER 27

Mickeys perspective

I get to the nearby hospital and help my Alina out of the car. She was really weak from all the crying, so I carried her up three flights of stairs to the third floor. I greet the nurse and ask her to direct us to Crystal. She does, and soon enough, we are standing there beside Crystal by her bedside. She looked as white as a ghost and unconscious. I go by her head as my Alina goes off and talks with the doctors. I mumble softly to her. "You are a beautiful girl," I say softly. "Choices can still be made; you are lovable. You are kind, smart, and funny too." I go on and on, saying positive affirmations until she pricks her eyes open when I say "I love you." "Do you?" She whispers to me softly. "I do, my love," I say. She leans up on her pillow. "Uncle, I had this strange dream..." "I know," I say. "It will be okay." She looks at me. "Were those things about me being pretty and lovable... were those comments really what you feel?" She asks. "My dearest niece, of course," I say. She gets up, smiles at me, and hugs me. She notices something on my sleeve. "Since when do you get tattoos, uncle?" She asks. I look at my arm.

There indeed was a tattoo, of two intertwining hearts, one with my name and one with Myla. I look back at her. "I guess now, apparently," I say. I have no idea how it got there. My Alina walks into the room. "Mommy! Crystal squeals and runs to my Alina with delight. My Alina just looks at me, her jaw dropping. "How the...." She mouths at me. I chuckle. Life is full of surprises I guess. The nurses look so surprised; one faints, one squeals and hugs my Alina and my niece. I guess a new family has begun. "Let's go home, girls, and to you nurses, you guys can come home with us. Let's celebrate."

Top of Form

CHAPTER 28

15 years later…..

I am sitting here at my niece's graduation. I have my newborn daughter and newly wedded wife beside me. Behind me is my sister Alina, who now works at her daughter's school, with a smile so big on her face, it was almost as big as the room. My niece comes down the stage with a boy by her side. "Mommy, uncle, I want you to meet my new boyfriend. His name is Julien." I looked at her then at Julien. "Well, nice to meet you!" I say. I shake hands with him; he seems pretty hesitant. "Let's go," my Alina said impatiently. "I need my coffee!" She says. My Alina kisses her boyfriend, says something, and races after her mom, leaving me and Julien alone. Julien stares at me and mumbles quietly. "When do I know it's the right time?" He asks.

Without hesitation I say this simple message, "Follow your heart, but make your choices wisely. There will always be a bridge between light and darkness, it is up to you which path you take."

Milton Keynes UK
Ingram Content Group UK Ltd.
UKHW021827190424
441445UK00018B/570